# Hello Kitty®
## Loves School!

Written by Elizabeth Smith
Illustrated by Jean Hirashima

HARRY N. ABRAMS, INC., PUBLISHERS

Now that summer vacation is over, Hello Kitty and her friends are back in school. Every day there are so many fun things to learn about and do!

On Monday, they have their first science class. Always curious, Fifi loves to look through a microscope and observe all sorts of interesting things very close up.

Cathy loves English class on Tuesday. She writes a sweet poem she shows only to Hello Kitty, one of her best friends.

On Wednesday, the friends have drama class. An imaginative storyteller, Thomas loves to write adventurous plays. And Mimmy loves to act in them!

Hello Kitty can hardly wait for Thursday's music class. She has practiced her scales carefully and learned to play many beautiful new songs.

Eat Healthy

Let's Play Soccer

A super athlete, Joey loves gym class on Friday the best. There, he gets to run fast, jump high, and somersault across the floor!

And what is their favorite part of the first week of school? Preparing for the first talent show of the year!

Hello Kitty and her friends are sure that this talent show will be a big success.

For the first act, Thomas and Mimmy perform a dramatic scene from Thomas's new play, "A Fantastic Adventure."

Act 1

The friends shout, "Bravo, Thomas! Brava, Mimmy!"

For the second act, Fifi mixes together a bubbling potion that smokes and turns all sorts of fascinating colors. "Eureka, Fifi!" exclaim the friends. "What have you discovered?"

Act 2

**And Act 3? Though Cathy is very shy, she stands in front of everyone and quietly recites her newest poem:**

*Cheerful poppies bob in the sun,*
*Until rainfall hushes them,*
*    one by one.*
*Then gray clouds flee from the sun*
*    shining bright,*
*And the poppies' bright petals open*
*    wide with delight.*

**Her friends applaud enthusiastically.**
**"Encore, encore!"**

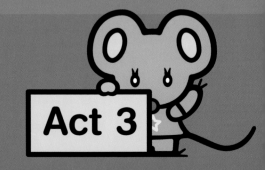

Act 3

For Act 4, Joey does two somersaults, three flips, and four cartwheels—a gymnastic feat! His friends agree that he scores a perfect "10."

And for the finale, Hello Kitty plays a charming waltz, and all of her friends dance together.

Thank you, Hello Kitty!

Finale

The friends agree that this was the best talent show ever . . . and that they can hardly wait for the next week of school!

Illustrations by Jean Hirashima
Text by Elizabeth Smith

Design by Celina Carvalho

Production Manager: Jonathan Lopes

Library of Congress Catalogingata:

Smith, E

Hello Kitty loves school / Elizab                                hima.

Summary: Hello Kitty and her friends take their favorite things about s                    r the first talent show of the school year.
ISBN 0-8109-4
[1. Talent shows—Fiction. 2. Schools—Fiction                              n, ill. II. Title.

PZ7.S64498
[E]—dc2
20040014

Printed and bound in China
10 9 8 7 6 5 4 3 2 1

ABRAMS

Harry N. Abrams, Inc.
100 Fifth Avenue
New York, NY 10011
www.abramsbooks.com

Abrams is a subsidiary of

LA MARTINIÈRE
GROUPE